THE
PUMPKINVILLE
MYSTERY

THE PUMPKINVILLE MYSTERY

BY BRUCE B. COLE
ILLUSTRATED BY JAMES WARHOLA

SIMON AND SCHUSTER BOOKS FOR YOUNG READERS   PUBLISHED BY SIMON & SCHUSTER INC., NEW YORK

Published by Simon and Schuster Books for Young Readers, A
Division of Simon & Schuster,
Inc., 1230 Avenue of the Ameri-
cas, New York, NY 10020

Simon and Schuster Books for
Young Readers is a trademark
of Simon & Schuster, Inc.

Designed by Rebecca Tachna
Manufactured in U.S.A.

10 9 8 7 6 5 4 3 2

10 9 8 7 6 5 4 3 2 pbk

Library of Congress Cataloging
in Publication Data

Cole, Bruce. The Pumpkinville
mystery. Summary: Through
the intercession of a mysteri-
ous stranger, good triumphs
over evil one Halloween.
[1. Halloween—Fiction] I.
Warhola, James, ill. II. Title.
PZ7.C673425Pu 1987 [E] 87-
2533 ISBN 0-671-66905-2 ISBN
0-671-66906-0 pbk.

To Mrs. Cole,
past, present and future
BBC

To my friends
and teachers
who have given me
support and inspiration.
JW

ONCE UPON A TIME, long before the horse and buggy had given way to the motor car, a town called Pumpkinville sprang up out in the prairies just a hoot and a holler to the right of Turkeytown and a stone's throw from the lower bend in the old Spooky River. Now, I am telling you this tale the way I heard it from my father who heard it from his father who heard it from his father who was there in Pumpkinville the very night the Pumpkinville mystery began.

Pumpkinville was founded by Hollis J. Goodbody and his wife Betsy who were forced to leave Turkeytown by greedy old Mr. Featherbed and the no-good members of the Turkeytown Council and Chamber of Commerce.

For many years, the people of Turkeytown had prospered by raising turkeys. The families who lived on the grassy knoll overlooking Turkeytown got richer than the others and built silos that reached to the sky. They filled their silos with corn until they were about to burst. These folks elected themselves the Turkeytown Council and Chamber of Commerce and began to buy up all the neighboring fields. Well, this did not seem to bother anyone except Hollis J. Goodbody. What Mr. Goodbody saw that no one else did was the Councilmen gobbling up all the fields where corn was grown—the corn to feed the turkeys the townsfolk raised. Mr. Goodbody realized that some day pretty soon everyone in Turkeytown would have to come to the Councilmen with hat in hand, begging for help to feed their turkeys. But no one else even suspected the Councilmen's plan.

The summer Hollis and Betsy Goodbody left Turkeytown it was so hot and dry you could see the bottom of the old Spooky River. The grass turned brown and the corn grew only as high as a grasshopper's knee.

Now remember, these Councilmen had stored up all of the turkey feed hereabouts. How much do you think they would charge for a small bag? Not much? Well, you guessed wrong. Half of everything you owned was what you would have to pay if you bought turkey feed from the Councilmen. And as the summer got hotter and drier, there was no one else to buy from.

Mr. Featherbed, the oldest and meanest of the Councilmen, had to hire three people to carry him around because he had so much gold and silver stuffed into the oversized pockets of his pants. Mr. Featherbed looked about one hundred and fifty years old with a pushed-in face that never smiled. Why, the wrinkles on his forehead were so deep you could grow corn in them. Anyhow, he sure wanted to get Mr. Hollis J. Goodbody and his wife out of town.

Now, during the summer dry spell, a stranger wandered into town one night. I don't know his name. I don't know that anyone got his name, but he asked everyone in town for shelter and something to eat. As I heard it, this stranger was kind of scary looking. He walked slowly and leaned on a big walking stick. You could hardly see his face because of the hooded coat he wore, but people said he had fire in his eyes and a mouth that went almost from one ear to the other. Everywhere he moved, he was followed by a cat as black as midnight with green eyes that could see right through you.

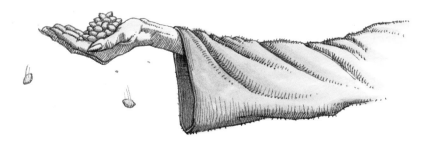

No one would help the stranger that night but Hollis J. Goodbody and Betsy. The stranger warmed himself by their blazing fire and shared their meal even though there was hardly enough to fill one plate. Before supper was over, the stranger suddenly stood up and said he had miles to go before his journey was over. He offered gold from a sack he pulled out of his hooded coat, but the Goodbodys refused it. So, instead, the stranger gave Hollis and Betsy a bag of seeds, which he said would someday be worth more than gold—if they did *exactly* what he said.

Come the harvest, he told them, they must move out onto the prairie just to the right of Turkeytown where they would find a field ready to be planted with pumpkins. But first, before they moved away, they had to plant three of the seeds right in Turkeytown. The Goodbodys didn't know anything about growing pumpkins and told the visitor so, but the stranger just embraced them both, saying he had searched long and far before finding the kindness they showed him. Then, without another word, he disappeared down the road as the moon was rushing away with the night.

As the stranger had told them, the Goodbodys planted the three seeds. The seeds must have been magic because each one grew as big as a barn in the twinkling of an eye. Summer waved goodbye to Turkeytown but left behind leaves that

were golden yellow and the Goodbodys' pumpkin field that was a ripe harvest orange. Hollis and Betsy shared their pumpkin harvest with everyone who had no food to eat. Pumpkin pie, pumpkin soup, pumpkin bread, pumpkin pudding. If it had not been for those pumpkins, the people of Turkeytown would have had to sell their homes, lock, stock and barrel, to the greedy Councilmen for turkey feed. But thanks to Hollis and Betsy, they could eat and they could feed their turkeys pumpkin seeds. This made Mr. Featherbed and the other Councilmen so angry they cooked up a dastardly scheme and laughed among themselves at how mean and low they could be.

On the first moonless night, the Councilmen, disguised as wolves and ghosts and creatures of the night, crept and crawled their way over to the Goodbodys' farm. While Hollis and Betsy slept, the Councilmen smashed the pumpkins to a pulp and stole all the seeds. Then they danced around a bonfire chanting rhymes of bogeymen and monsters.

Roused from sleep, the frightened people of Turkeytown peered through curtained windows in time only to see long shadows fleeing, but eerie shrieks came from the woods for the rest of the night.

While the Councilmen were celebrating their victory and counting their stolen pumpkin seeds, Hollis J. Goodbody and his wife Betsy pulled up stakes. By the time the Councilmen found out, they had moved. As they had been told by the stranger, they moved a stone's throw away just to the right of Turkeytown and were growing more pumpkins.

Some of the townspeople went with the Goodbodys and helped found a new town they called Pumpkinville. They built the houses of Pumpkinville in a circle around the pumpkin patch and celebrated with the first pumpkin pie bake-off ever

recorded. Fiddlers and jug band musicians played and everyone ate pumpkin pie and danced. Best of all was the long distance pumpkin-seed-spitting contest which became famous in these here parts.

Folks began leaving Turkeytown for Pumpkinville as quickly as leaves falling from a tree. Too bad for that wicked Mr. Featherbed and his band of thieves! Who would put gold in the Councilmen's pockets now? That scheming Mr. Featherbed figured that if a nasty plan worked once, it could work again. The Councilmen marked their calendars for October 31 so that the harvest would be complete.

Now I'm not saying you have to believe the events I'm about to unfold, but you can find the truth in every young child's heart on Halloween night.

Well, sir, the Turkeytown Council and Chamber of Commerce sure picked one scary, misty, pitch-black night to go for a visit, especially a not-so-friendly visit. The road between the two towns was wide and open, but to avoid being seen, the seven Councilmen led by Mr. Featherbed crept over the slope of a hogbacked ridge and through a narrow winding woods full of hoot owls, bats, and coyotes.

Hollis had spent a long day harvesting and stacking pumpkins in a circle. He was tired. As the sun was setting he hunkered down by the tree stump on the edge of the pumpkin patch to watch the last rays of the sun shine on the field and dozed off with a smile on his face.

Night had fallen as the seven Councilmen snuck into Hollis' pumpkin patch with their gunny sacks. Mr. Featherbed picked up a pumpkin in each hand and was just about to smash them together like cymbals when a black cat with piercing green eyes leaped into the center of the pumpkin circle. It hissed and arched and bristled every black hair. Through a thick mist, a hooded figure moved slowly toward the cowering seven, and with each step, their seven heartbeats quickened until they beat like tom-toms.

The hooded stranger stretched out his willowy arm, and immediately the largest pumpkin began to shake and grow. Eyes and a mouth with jagged teeth appeared while a blazing fire burst forth from the pumpkin's belly. Seven vines snaked their way from the pumpkin to the Councilmen and wrapped them in a cold embrace, pulling them closer and closer to the ever-growing pumpkin.

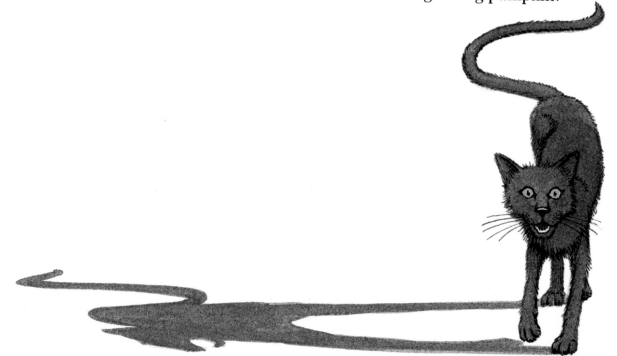

Mr. Featherbed yelled, "Save me," and a chorus of wolves in the woods howled—and woke Hollis from what he must have thought was a dream. He had goose bumps all over, but up he jumped into the circle of pumpkins and stood toe to toe with the hooded figure.

"You must stop now," Hollis said. "Let them go home."

The hooded figure pulled a handful of crushed seeds out of his cloak, and with a flick of his wrist scattered them in a shower. The vines released the Councilmen like spinning tops and sent them running home as fast as their legs could carry them.

In another instant the black cat had disappeared with its master, leaving Hollis alone in the middle of the pumpkin circle.

When Hollis got home to Betsy, he put a pumpkin with a carved-out face in their window with a candle glowing inside to keep the spirits of the night from their door.

The Councilmen promised each other never to tell anyone how frightened they had been that night. Of course, that's how legends begin.

From that year on, near the end of October, all the people of Pumpkinville carved faces on their pumpkins just as Hollis had done and invited the children to go door to door for candy and other treats. And the idea spread from Pumpkinville to just about every town. You probably have glowing pumpkins in your town at Halloween time too. Well, now you know where the whole thing started. At least that's how I learned the story from my daddy's grandpa.

The End.